Steve Hartley is many things: author, astronaut, spy, racing-car driver, trapeze-artist and vampire-hunter. His hobbies include puddle-diving and hamster-wrestling and he was voted 'Coolest Dude of the Year' for five years running by *Seriously Cool* magazine. Steve is 493 years old, lives in a golden palace on top of a dormant volcano in Lancashire and never, EVER, tells fibs. You can find out more about Steve on his extremely silly website: www.stevehartley.net

Also by Steve Hartley

The DANNY BAKER RECORD BREAKER series

The World's Biggest Bogey

The World's Awesomest Air-Barf

The World's Loudest Armpit Fart

The World's Stickiest Earwax

The World's Itchiest Pants

The World's Windiest Baby

Coming soon:

Oliver Fibbs and the Giant Boy-Munching Bugs

www.stevehartley.net

ILLUSTRATED BY BERNICE LUM

MACMILLAN CHILDREN'S BOOKS

First published 2013 by Macmillan Children's Books
a division of Macmillan Publishers Limited
20 New Wharf Road, London N1 9RR
Basingstoke and Oxford
Associated companies throughout the world
www.panmacmillan.com

ISBN 978-1-4472-2023-7

1 3 5 7 9 8 6 4 2

A CIP catalogue record for this book is available from the British Library.

Printed and bound by CPI Group (UK) Ltd, Croydon CR0 4YY

For my three girls:

Rosie, Connie and Louise

(SH)

For my brother, Charles . . . much xo

(BL)

CHAPTER 1

WHAT IF . . . ?

My fingers were stiff, the muscles in my arms ached with tiredness, but I had to go on. I'd been holding up the **HUGE, heavy** book, *The Complicated Scale Drawings of Nineteenth-Century Engineers* by Professor Wilberforce J. Pilkington, for over an hour. I couldn't put it down – it was too exciting! My heart battered against my ribs. How was it going to end?

I turned to the last page of my new comic, ***Agent Q and the ZYGON CONSPIRACY***, which I'd sneakily hidden inside the book when nobody was looking.

Agent Q was in terrible danger. The Zygon leader, General Durg, had captured Q and strapped him into a machine that was sucking all the thoughts out of his brain, including vital secrets about the Earth's defence shield.

DURG'S LIZARD BRAIN GOES, 'POP!'

I closed my comic and sighed. Why can't I save the Earth from alien lizard-

men and then go for a strawberry milkshake? Why can't I be cool? Why can't I be **BRILLIANT**?

The only **BRILLIANT** thing about me is my family:

My mum, Charlotte Pomeroy Templeton Tibbs, is a **BRILLIANT** brain surgeon. She saves people's lives.

My dad, Granville Fitzwilliam Templeton Tibbs, is a **BRILLIANT** architect. He designs award-winning buildings.

My big twin sisters, Emma Letitia Templeton Tibbs, and Gemma Darcy Templeton Tibbs, are **BRILLIANT** dancers. They go to a top ballet school.

And my little brother, Algernon Montgomery Templeton Tibbs, is **BRILLIANT** at maths. He's only eight years old, but he already goes to university, *and* he's the National Chess Champion. + ÷ =

Last (and least) there's me,

Oliver Ranulph Templeton Tibbs.

I'm **BRILLIANT** at . . .

- sitting in my bedroom reading **Agent Q** comics, and . . .

- sitting at the back of a theatre while my sisters dance around in their tutus, and . . .
- sitting in the car while Algy is taken to a chess tournament.

Just then, I was being *fantastically* **BRILLIANT** at sitting in one corner of a big dusty room while my little brother played chess against ten people at the same time. All the players were thinking hard about their next moves. It was as quiet as the underground bunker in ***Agent Q and the*** *Secret Spy School*, when **Agent Q** knocks out the enemy agents with sleeping gas from a capsule in his shoe.

Now I'd finished my comic, I was bored, bored, bored, bored, **bored!**

I looked around the room, and began to wonder . . .

WHAT IF . . . Algy's opponents were all alien swamp beasts in disguise, ready to take over the world if he lost just one game?

WHAT IF . . . Algy's chair was booby-trapped with a lethal alien STINK BOMB, set to go off if it looked as if he'd beat them all?

WHAT IF . . . I was the only person who knew?

Dad crept over, interrupting me just as I was about to go into action. I slammed the big, **BORING** book closed so he wouldn't see the comic inside. The sound boomed and echoed in the huge room, and about forty people all went, **'Shhhhhhhhhh!'** at the same time (which is probably what a lethal alien STINK BOMB going off would sound like).

'Are you enjoying Professor Pilkington's book?' he whispered.

'I can't put it down,' I whispered back.

Dad beamed with pleasure. 'Algy's winning every match,' he said.

'Good,' I replied. 'The fate of the world depends on it.'

Dad frowned. 'What?'

'Er . . . never mind. Can I have a Snik-Snak chocolate bar from the machine?'

'Look!' said Dad. 'Two more of his opponents have given up! Algy's already won FOUR games! He's amazing!' Dad thrust some coins into my hand for the Snik-Snak, and tiptoed away to watch my **BRILLIANT** little brother.

I sighed, and placed the book on the seat next to me. Making me read *The Complicated Scale Drawings of Nineteenth-Century Engineers* was just Mum and Dad's latest desperate attempt to find out what I'm *actually* good at. So far, I've had:

- golf lessons (I kept missing the ball)
- tennis lessons (I kept hitting the net)
- horse-riding lessons (I kept falling off – I even fell off a Shetland pony)
- drawing lessons (I couldn't draw a wiggly line)
- piano lessons (I couldn't even play 'Chopsticks') and
- singing lessons (I sounded like a donkey with bellyache).

I've been forced to read books about atomic physics, economics and computer programming, when all I really want to do is read comics.

I think reading **Agent Q** comics is

interesting, but no one else does. And when Monday mornings at school come round, that's Very Bad News, because Monday mornings at school are **SHOW AND TELL** time (or, as I call it, PAIN AND TORTURE time).

CHAPTER 2

PAIN AND TORTURE

It was Monday morning, and Miss Wilkins began to go through the register. She called out Bobby Bragg's name, and he stood up in front of the class. *Here we go*, I thought as my heart started to sink.

'What did you do at the weekend, Bobby?'

'I got my black belt in karate.'

'How wonderful!'

Bobby then swivelled and jumped in the air,

kicking, punching and chopping, making loud, `Aiyah!', `Ho!' and `Ha!' noises as he demolished an army of invisible attackers.

Next, Miss Wilkins called up Hattie Hurley. I knew this would be good.

`What did you do at the weekend, Hattie?'

`I trounced the opposition at the Regional Spelling Bee Championships.'

`How thrilling!' said Miss Wilkins.

My best friend, Peaches Mazimba, pulled a dictionary out of her bag and looked up the word `trounced'.

'It means she won easily,' she whispered to me.

Then Hattie showed us how she did it. Miss Wilkins asked her to spell 'claustrophobic' and she got it right! (*I* had to look it up to write it down just now).

As Melody Nightingale walked to the front of the class, my shoulders were drooping so much they nearly touched my knees.

'And what did you do at the weekend, Melody?'

'On Saturday, I sang the national anthem at the big football match.'

'How fantastic!'

Melody then showed us all her amazing singing voice, warbling beautifully through the whole anthem once again, but this time without a massive marching band backing her, *obviously.*

Nearly *everyone* had done something interesting over the weekend. Even Peaches had taken part in the Mayor's Parade, dressed up as a bedbug on the town council's pest-extermination float. She showed us a photo. You couldn't really see her properly because she was curled up underneath a duvet, and stuck behind a giant can of 'DOCTOR DOOM' bug killer, but I thought she looked

awesome.

When Miss Wilkins finally called out my name, I sighed and dragged myself to the front of the class.

'What did *you* do at the weekend, Oliver?'

I squeezed my eyes shut, desperately searching my brain for something good to tell. 'We had pizza for dinner on Saturday.'

An explosion of deafening laughter from the rest of the class smashed into me. Miss Wilkins smiled as though I was an abandoned puppy that had been left tied to a lamppost in the rain.

'How lovely!' she said. 'Was it a tasty pizza, Oliver?'

'Yes, miss!' I replied. 'It had FOUR toppings! And the slices were so juicy and floppy I had to eat them like this . . .'

I showed the class my **EXTREME PIZZA-EATING TECHNIQUE,**

putting my head back and pretending to dangle the imaginary wobbly slice over my open mouth.

The laughter rolled over me like a huge tsunami wave.

Miss Wilkins was trying not to laugh too. 'Well, well . . . four toppings . . .' she said. 'Fancy that . . .'

Peaches tried to help me out, like she always does, but it just made things worse. 'What toppings did you have, Ollie?' she asked.

'Pepperoni, onions, green peppers *and* red peppers,' I replied.

'Pepperoni's too hot for me,' she said. 'You're very brave.'

'He's very **BORING!**' shouted Bobby Bragg, doing a loud pretend yawn.

This time, the laughter seemed to pick me up and slam me hard against the whiteboard.

I bowed my head and scuttled back to my place, my face hot and my heart tapping out a rat-a-tat rhythm inside my chest.

It's the same every week: I don't do anything exciting, so I never have anything good to talk about. A couple of months ago, I thought I'd finally got something interesting to **SHOW AND TELL**.

I told the class I'd been to the dentist and found a copy of ***Agent Q and the Beasts from the Deep*** in the waiting room. I held up the

comic to show everyone, and explained that the dentist had let me keep it.

Bobby Bragg shouted, 'Nobody reads those stupid **Agent Q** comics any more. You're a geek, Tibbs!'

I ignored him and carried on. I told the class that I'd collected 439 different comics, and when I found a copy of the incredibly rare ***Agent Q and the*** *Doomsday Scrolls*, I'd have the full set.

Miss Wilkins said, 'How interesting!' and asked which was my favourite.

'***Agent Q and the GHOST WARRIORS OF THE NILE***,' I replied. 'I've read that one twenty-nine times.'

'You're a DABKid, Tibbs,' shouted Bobby. '**Dull And Boring.** In fact, if *you* were in

a comic book, you'd be **DABMAN!**'

The class ROARED with laughter, and some of them began to chant, '**DABMAN! DABMAN!**' over and over again.

Miss Wilkins gave Bobby a playtime detention and docked three SHINE TIME points from his score for name-calling, but it made no difference to me – the new name stuck.

You see, everyone in my class knows it; everyone in my school knows it; I bet even Rambo, the Year 6 hamster, knows it . . .

It's OK if you're one of the ***SAS KIDS*** – the Super And Special ones – you have amazing things to **SHOW AND TELL**. The ***SAS KIDS*** have special meetings after school. They go on their own special trips to science museums and have special days out to visit universities. They probably even sleep in a Super And Special way.

But what about the rest of us, the ***DAB KIDS***? What have we got to talk about?

Zip. Zero. Nothing.

At least I'm not alone – there are others in my class who are almost as **Dull And Boring** as I am.

Peaches would love to climb mountains with her dad and big brother, but she gets dizzy if she stands on a chair.

Leon Curley would love to be a world-champion wrestler like his hero Steel Kong, but Leon's so small and quiet he'd have to compete in the weedyweight division.

Millie Dangerfield would love to be a Hollywood film star like her big idol Ritzy Savoy, but Millie's so nervous she got stage fright playing a sheep in the school nativity play.

Being ordinary doesn't bother Peaches. 'Why do you want to be a **SAS** KID?' she once asked me.

'I don't,' I replied. 'It's my mum and dad. They want me to be **BRILLIANT** at something, like the rest of my family.'

'But then you'd have to sit with Bobby Bragg,' she said, wrinkling up her nose as though she'd got a whiff of a BAD SMELL. 'Why would they want you to do *that*?'

Peaches heaved her Eco Warrior shoulder bag on to her lap, and undid the straps. As she flung the bag open, I peeked inside at all her neatly arranged stuff. There were pockets and zipped-up compartments, Velcro straps holding pens, and clips with keys and lucky charms hanging from them.

She caught me staring, and raised one eyebrow. 'A place for everything, and everything in its place, my mum says. If I need something, I know exactly where it is.'

'What have you got in there?'

She began to list some of the items:

- ✔ a pen-torch, in case there's a power cut
- ✔ a compass, in case I get lost
- ✔ a stopwatch, in case I need to time something
- ✔ a spare pen, in case I lose my best one
- ✔ a notebook, in case I need to make notes – obviously
- ✔ a pound coin, in case I need money . . .
- ✔ a first-aid kit, in case anyone needs first aid
- ✔ a stapler and staples
- ✔ paper clips
- ✔ rubber bands
- ✔ emergency supplies of fruity Yummy-Gum Drops
- ✔ big sunglasses, in case I need a disguise

She went to close the flap, but I saw something else in the bag. 'Why have you got a pair of socks in there?'

'They're spares,' Peaches replied. 'Just in case.' She stuck her chin out defiantly. 'I'm not Super And Special, but I'm ready for anything.'

I sighed. 'I'm not Super And Special, and I'm ready for *nothing.*' ☹

CHAPTER 3

WAITING

On the following Friday afternoon, I was sitting at my desk doing a tricky long-division sum, when our headteacher, Mrs Broadside, rushed into the classroom and whispered something to Miss Wilkins.

`Oliver, pack your bag and get your coat,´ said Mrs Broadside. `Your mother has been called into hospital to do an emergency operation. She´s going to pick you

up on the way and take you with her.'

Now THIS was exciting! I hardly ever got to go to the hospital with my mum. I could see everyone was really interested as I grabbed my bag and dashed out of the classroom behind Mrs Broadside. Bobby Bragg *definitely* looked jealous. Luckily, school's quite close to the hospital, and a minute later Mum pulled up at the gates. I noticed Bobby Bragg staring out of the window, so I ***HURLED*** my bag into the back of the car, ***DIVED*** in next to Mum and we ***WHIZZED*** off down the road, just like **Agent Q** when he was after the robbers in ***Agent Q and the* GOLD BULLION BANK RAIDERS.**

Mum explained that there was no one at home to look after me. Our Italian nanny, Constanza, had gone to see ace rapper **DOOP DIGGY DOOP** that night, Dad was away at a bank-designing conference, my sisters were rehearsing for a big performance of *Swan Lake* and Algy was at a training camp with the National Junior Genius Squad, so Mum only had me to worry about.

THIS was cool. I began to wonder . . .

WHAT IF . . . Mum's patient is the world's leading expert on alien invasion?

Actually, her patient was a plumber from the Mr Fixit Building Company. Mum said she'd asked him to put a new toilet in our bathroom when he was feeling better.

'I brought *The Complicated Scale Drawings of Nineteenth-Century Engineers* for you to read while I'm working,' she said. 'Your dad told me you were really enjoying it. Maybe you're going to be

a world-famous engineer some day, Oliver.'

I was *totally* **BRILLIANT** at sitting for hours in the hospital waiting room that afternoon. Luckily, my comic was still hidden inside the book. I managed to read ***Agent Q and the ZYGON CONSPIRACY*** for the second time, and it was just as good, if not better, than the first time.

When I finished, I ate a Snik-Snak and a satsuma. Then I stared out of the waiting-room window for a while and counted the vehicles in the car park. There were:

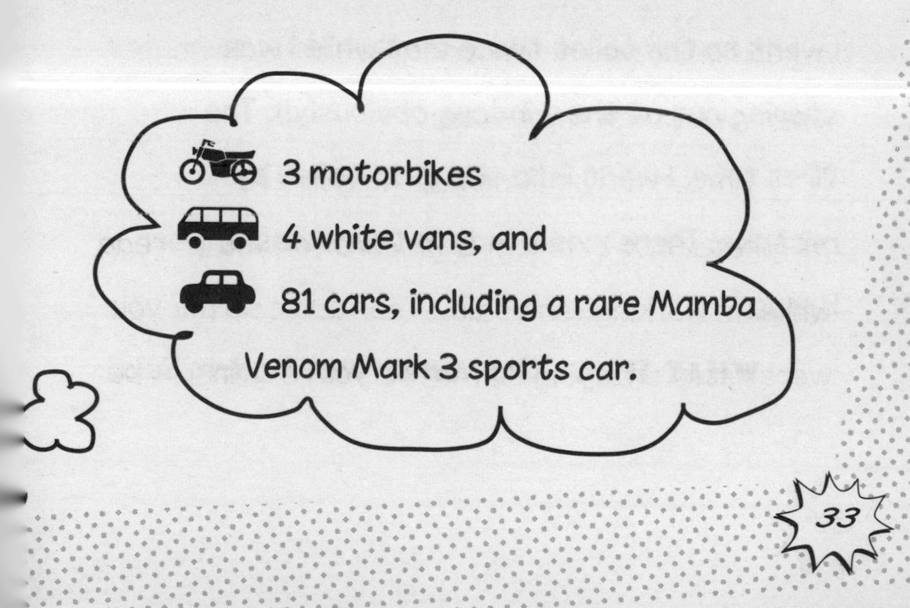

WHAT IF . . . the Mamba Venom Mark 3 sports car could transform into a spaceship?

I waited . . . and waited . . . and waited . . . I went to the toilet twice (not while I was staring out of the window, obviously!). The first time, I went into the girls' toilet by mistake. There was a lady in there washing her hands.

WHAT IF . . . the woman was Madam Sula,

the famous ***INTERGALACTIC SPACE SPY***,

come to stop Mum from doing the operation?

'Eek!' shouted the lady.

'Sorry!' I shouted, and ran out.

Definitely *not* an Intergalactic Space Spy.

I bumped into one of the hospital cleaners as I raced back into the corridor. I remembered her from the last time Mum left me hanging around at the hospital.

'Hi, Betty,' I said. 'Wrong toilet.'

She laughed and offered me a jelly baby.

I chose a red one, because they're my favourite.

'Do you want to help me tidy my store cupboard while you're waiting for your mum to finish?' asked Betty.

WHAT IF . . . Betty was a secret agent looking for Madam Sula, and the cupboard was full of government files and alien weapons?

EXTREMELY HUSH-HUSH! KEEP OUT!

But when Betty opened the door the room was just full of cleaning stuff: bottles of disinfectant, boxes of rubber gloves and towers of toilet rolls. She noticed that a mop and

bucket were missing – we searched everywhere, and I eventually found them behind the door in the gents' loos.

When we'd finished, Betty said I could have *all* the red jelly babies as a reward for helping.

Eventually, Mum finished the operation and took me home for supper.

'How did it go?' I asked as we left the hospital. 'Did you have to cut great big lumps of his brain out?'

'Oliver! Please . . .'

'Did you have to do a total brain transplant?'

'Oliver! I really don't think . . .'

'Did you have to do a total *head* transplant – cut his head off and sew on a completely new one?'

'Oliver, you can be quite disgusting sometimes.'

I gave up, folded my arms and sighed. 'What's for supper?'

Mum grinned. 'Brains on toast!'

CHAPTER 4

SHOW AND TELL

Next Monday, it was the same as ever: the **SAS** KIDS had all had exciting weeks and weekends, and the **DAB** KIDS hadn't.

Bobby Bragg had climbed Mount Badrock with the Cub Scouts.

Jamie Ryder had broken his thumb flying off his BMX bike on the final bend in the County Finals.

Toby Hadron told us how he had invented

a mega-powerful electromagnet. He'd brought it with him, and as he switched it on dozens of metal objects like paper clips, drawing pins and the spoon in Miss Wilkins's coffee cup began ***flying*** across the room. Millie Dangerfield's glasses shot off her nose and clattered into the metal end of the magnet too!

The **DAB KIDS** had all done zip. Zero. Nothing.

Miss Wilkins called out my name. 'Now, we all know that Oliver had an exciting trip to the hospital with his mum on Friday, don't we, class?' She smiled at me. 'Why don't you tell everyone what happened, Oliver?'

I stood up and faced the class. 'My mum had to do an emergency operation,' I said.

Miss Wilkins nodded enthusiastically. 'Now *that's* interesting, Oliver! What did **YOU** do while you were there?'

My stomach churned and twisted as I scanned the wall of faces. I saw Bobby Bragg grinning at me, expecting to have a good laugh, as usual.

I don't know why I said what I said. It just came out of my mouth before I could stop it.

'It was a life or death brain operation . . . and I saved the patient's life!'

Some of the kids gasped. The look of surprise on Miss Wilkins's face was excellent! Her eyebrows shot so high they nearly flew off her face, and her mouth opened and shut **SO** many times she looked like my goldfish, Tango.

'Oliver,' she spluttered, 'that can't be true!'

I was in trouble. Should I admit it was a ***BIG FAT FIB***, and get laughed out of the classroom? I wondered . . .

WHAT IF . . . all the other doctors and nurses had got stuck in a massive traffic jam on the motorway, and couldn't get to the hospital in time?

`Mum had to operate on the brain of a top rocket scientist called Professor Hugo van Boomberg,´ I told the class. `His brain had swelled up with all the secret thoughts inside it, and his head was about to **EXPLODE!**

unless she did the operation straight away.'

Bobby Bragg snorted with laughter. 'Liar! Liar! Your pants are on fire!'

'DEFENDERS OF PLANET EARTH SECURITY?' laughed Hattie Hurley. 'D-O-P-E-S spells dopes!'

Deafening shrieks of laughter boomed in my ears, as though a funny-bomb had exploded in the classroom. Why hadn't I come up with a different name? It was too late now; I carried on quickly with my story.

'We scrubbed up, and Mum cut the top of the scientist's head off with a huge can opener . . .'

'EUGHHHHH!' groaned the class.

'As she lifted the professor's skull off, there was a sound – hissssssssssss – like someone letting air out of a tyre,' I told them. 'And there was the brain, all red and wet and wrinkly, bulging out of his open head.'

DABMAN DIVES ACROSS THE OPERATING TABLE AND GRABS THE WOBBLING, SLIMY BALL JUST BEFORE IT HITS THE FLOOR . . .

'EUGHHHHH!' groaned the class once more.

Hattie Hurley's face went a strange greeny-grey colour.

I was enjoying myself now, and I could see that Bobby Bragg was really cross that someone was doing a more interesting **SHOW AND TELL** than him.

'Brains aren't red, they don't fall out of heads and they don't wobble,' he sneered. 'I've seen them on telly.'

'Well, this one did,' I replied. 'Because . . . because . . . this brain . . . was *alive*!'

The class gasped again.

'Really, Oliver!' said Miss Wilkins.

'The brain wriggled from my hands and jumped on to the scientist's chest,' I said. 'It sat there, wobbling like a big, lumpy raspberry jelly, then suddenly sprang on to the floor.'

'How could it move?' asked Toby Hadron.

Tricky question. Think! Think! Think! I stared at Toby, and put my hands into my pockets. Luckily, I'd brought a couple of jelly babies to munch on at break, and the feel of the soft, squishy sweet sparked more pictures in my head.

'The brain changed shape,' I replied. 'It grew a body, and arms and legs. It looked like a **slimy**, red jelly baby, but with a thin black slit for a mouth, and two evil yellow eyes.'

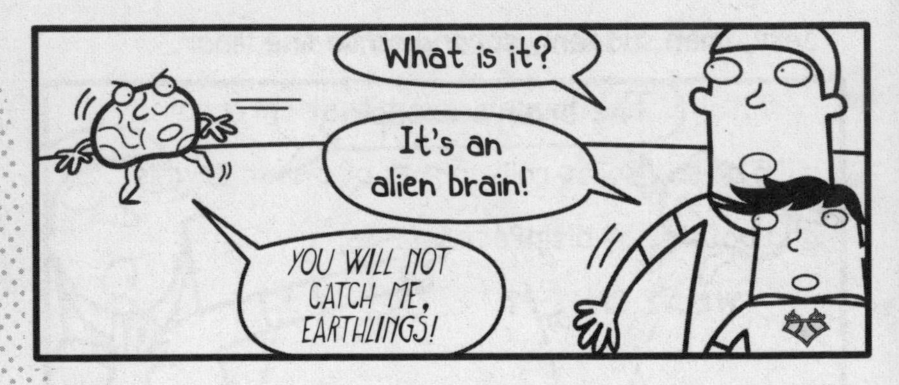

I did the brain's voice in a creepy, croaky, alien-type growl, which made the class giggle.

How was I going to get out of this? Miss Wilkins sat there smiling at me. She *knew* I was making it all up.

'How big was it?' asked Peaches, trying to help me out.

'Not as big as this fib!' yelled Bobby Bragg. The class giggled.

'The brain was brain-sized – obviously,' I said, but I was panicking now.

I tried to remember what was in the hospital, and I thought about the storeroom, with all the toilet rolls, boxes of paper towels and bottles of disinfectant.

WHAT IF . . . ?

The classroom was hushed now: the kids were hooked on my ***Big Fat Fib.***

But what now? I remembered the girls' toilet.

WHAT IF . . .?

LADIES
Madam Sula!
We meet again, DABMan. You may be the most Daring And Brave boy on Earth, but you will not stop us!
SULA FIRES HER RAY BLASTER AT DABMAN. HE REFLECTS THE RAYS WITH A BUCKET. SULA'S BODY MELTS INTO A PUDDLE OF SLIME.
ARGHHHHHHHHHHHHHHH!
DABMAN DIVES FOR THE BRAIN, BUT IT BOUNCES INTO ONE OF THE CUBICLES.

I WILL RETURN, EARTHLINGS!

'What were all those brains doing in the jars?' asked Bobby Bragg.

'They're more aliens,' I replied.

'But why were they there?' he said.

'I don't know,' I answered. 'I didn't ask them!'

'And what happened to the rocket scientist your mum operated on?' asked Toby Hadron. 'How did he survive without his brain?'

This was a *really* tricky one. 'Mum did a brain transplant,' I said. 'She put an old monkey brain into his head, and glued his skull back on. He can't work on rockets any more, but he *can* swing from a tree and eat a banana at the same time.'

Miss Wilkins coughed. 'Well, what an interesting Friday afternoon you had, Oliver.

And what have you brought to show the class, to prove that this happened?'

Uh-oh . . . I hadn't thought of that. I could feel my face getting hot and flushed. Then I remembered the jelly baby in my pocket.

I squashed it between my fingers and thumb, then held out the red, squishy mess on the palm of my hand.

'This,' I said, 'is a lump of the brain that fell off as it bashed into the toilet door.'

'EUGHHHHH!' groaned the class again.

Hattie Hurley threw up.

Bobby Bragg shouted, 'You're not Oliver Tibbs, you're **OLIVER FIBBS!**'

CHAPTER 5

GROUNDED

Miss Wilkins was a bit cross about my story, and me showing the jelly-baby-brain-blob that made Hattie Hurley sick. She took two SHINE TIME points from my score (which meant I now had -1) and gave me playtime detention.

My first detention ever! I was getting more interesting by the day.

The empty classroom echoed with the loud

ticking of the clock, the rustling of paper as Miss Wilkins marked our history workbooks and the scratching of my **Agent Q** pen as I wrote down the ***Big Fat Fib.***

At lunchtime, Peaches slid her lunch tray on to the table and sat down next to me. 'Ollie, what were you doing at **SHOW AND TELL**?'

'I couldn't help it,' I explained. 'The fib just popped out.'

'Well, why didn't you just pop it back in again?'

'Once I'd started, I couldn't stop,' I replied. 'It was great being ***DABman***, the Dynamic And Brave

alien brain-chaser. I enjoyed playtime detention too. Miss Wilkins made me write down my fib – I mean my story. It was fun.'

'Detention's not supposed to be fun,' said Peaches. 'It's supposed to be a punishment.' She rolled her eyes at me, and shook her head. 'There's no need to make things up; you should just be happy being Oliver Tibbs.'

'But Bobby's right: I'm **Dull And Boring.**'

'You're not! You're a trillion times nicer than him,' she said, '*and* you eat spicy pizza.'

After school, our nanny Constanza arrived to pick me up, ten minutes late (as usual), shouting, '*Il traffico!* **Beep-beep! honk-honk!** *Terribile!*'

She sat with Miss Wilkins and they spoke in whispers. I caught the occasional word of their conversation: naughty . . . worrying . . . mamma mia! and pork chop. Every now and then, they would stop talking and just look at me. Constanza was frowning like she was in training for the World Frowning Championships.

She marched me to the car, babbling all the time in Italian. My twin sisters Emma and Gemma were in the back seat, their long blonde hair scraped back into tight knots on the tops of their heads. As usual, they were too busy talking about ballet stuff to say hello.

They do that all the time. They're like one person in two bodies: they look alike, they dress

alike and they talk alike. They do everything and go everywhere together, and they gang up on me together.

As we made our way home, Constanza spoke to the twins in Italian. She *can* speak

English, but she's not allowed to. Mum and Dad say that if she only speaks to us in Italian it'll help us learn another language. It's working with my brother and sisters, but I can't understand a word she says.

She must have told Emma and Gemma about my **BIG FAT FIB**, because they stared at me like I'd let off a **STINK BOMB** in the car.

'*We've* never had detention!' said Emma.

'*We've* never got into trouble!' added Gemma.

Then they got bored with me and changed the subject – back to ballet, of course.

'Eugenia Lovelace's *grand plié* is anything but grand if you ask me,' said Emma, turning back to Gemma. 'She bends like an old woman.'

'Her *grand jeté* is even worse,' agreed Gemma. 'She jumps like an old sheep.'

When we got home, Mum and Dad were terribly worried about me. We sat around the kitchen table for ages while they grilled me about why I'd fibbed.

'Why, Oliver, why?' asked Dad.

I shrugged. 'It was fun.'

'I hope you're not **Going Bad**, like that Peter Cowper,' said Mum. (That's how she said it – like the words had capital letters.)

Mum and Dad are always talking about Peter Cowper. He's the boy next door. He started out Good, but then **Went Bad**, and turned to a life of crime, paying two Super And Special kids three Snik-Snak bars every week to do all his homework for him. Mum says Peter

is 'a **Tearaway**' and 'a **Difficult Teenager**'. He's got millions of pimples and he wears his cap back to front, so I suppose he must be.

'It could be even worse than that,' said Dad, giving Mum a meaningful look.

Mum gasped. 'You don't mean . . . ?'

Dad nodded. 'Oliver could turn out like Black Jack Tibbs.'

'Who's he?' I asked.

'The black sheep of our family,' answered Dad. 'He lived over two hundred years ago. He was a vagabond and a villain, and we don't like to talk about him. When he died, Black Jack vowed that he would haunt this family forever,

and since that day every generation of Tibbs has produced a **Bad Un**.'

Dad stared at me with wide, worried eyes. 'Maybe this time, Oliver, the **Bad Un** is you.'

I didn't say anything, but I thought, *Cool*. I couldn't wait to tell Peaches about Dad's theory.

Mum glanced at the clock. 'I've got to go,' she said. 'I can't keep Madame Snooté waiting – she's making Princess Chelsea's wedding dress when the twins' swan costumes are done.'

Dad stood up. 'Is that the time?' he said. 'Algy will be late for his chess match.'

'Oliver,' said Mum sternly, pointing a finger at me, 'you are not to **Go Bad**. You

are **OFFICIALLY GROUNDED** for a week as punishment for being put in detention.'

Emma and Gemma were standing in the doorway, and I heard them gasp.

'*We've* never been grounded,' whispered Emma.

'*We've* never **Gone Bad**,' added Gemma.

Mum and Dad picked up their car keys and rushed out of the house, with my brother and sisters hurrying behind.

Constanza stared at me and shook her head. '*Cattivo!*' she said.

I thought this was odd, because we haven't got a cat.

'I say bad boy in Italian,' she explained, pinching my cheek. 'You want some ice cream?'

Constanza got some raspberry ripple from the freezer and we ate it straight out of the tub. Then we sat together on the sofa and read **Agent Q and the** ***CAVE OF THE RED SCORPION.*** Constanza said it was much better than the **GUARDIANS OF THE GALAXY** comics she used to read when she was a kid.

Actually, being grounded was great – it meant that I didn't have to sit for hours watching my brother or sisters doing all their Super And Special things. I was *forced* to stay in my room every evening, which gave me loads of time to read my **Agent Q** comics.

On Tuesday evening, there was a massive storm. All the lights went out, so I turned on my torch and carried on reading. I was halfway through ***Agent Q and the* CIRCUS OF HORRORS**, and had just got to the part where **Agent Q** fights the two-headed clawman. With all the thunder and lightning going on around me, it was **awesome**!

WHAT IF . . . it wasn't thunder and lightning, but a battle between the D.O.P.E.S. star-fighters and the invading Zygon fleet?

On Wednesday evening, I was just settling down to read *Agent Q and the* ***GHOST WARRIORS OF THE NILE*** for the thirtieth time, when Emma and Gemma burst into my room.

'What have you done to our ballet slippers?' they wailed, each waving a pair of pink pumps at me.

'You could have ruined our *pas de deux*!' yelled Emma.

'You could have destroyed our *pas de chat*!' yelled Gemma.

I gawped. I gasped. I giggled. Their feet were covered in glowing **green slime**.

'Well . . . ?' they demanded.

'I haven't touched your ballet slippers,' I replied. 'And what's that on your feet?'

'As if you don't know!' said Emma.

'As if you didn't do it!' said

Gemma, snatching a pot of **Slimy Stuff** from the desk under my bedroom window, and yanking off the lid.

'Ha!' they cried together.

The pot was empty.

'It wasn't me!' I told them.

'You've **Gone Bad**,' said Emma.

'You've **Gone *Really* Bad**,' said Gemma, hurling the empty pot at me.

'It wasn't me!' I protested.

'Do anything like this again, and you're toast,' said Emma.

'Do anything like this again, and you're *beans* on toast!' said Gemma.

They turned and stomped out, leaving behind a trail of **green slime** on the bedroom carpet.

'But . . . it wasn't me,' I repeated to the empty room.

WHAT IF . . . the **Slimy Stuff** was actually a tub of mutant bacteria that had been blasted by radioactivity, and was spreading

Bothersome Itchy Foot Rot

disease across the world?

FOOT ROT!

OH NO!

On Thursday evening, I cleaned out the goldfish bowl. It was getting so green and gungy, I could hardly see Tango swimming round and round inside.

WHAT IF . . .

WHAT IF . . .

WHAT IF . . . it was just a filthy fishbowl?

THE GLOWING SLIME
CREEPS INTO A
BALLET SLIPPER.
SLIMY STUFF
ARGHHH!
It's the end of the world!
WE'LL NEVER DANCE AGAIN!

Just as I'd finished, and put Tango back in the clean bowl, there was a knock at my bedroom door. It was Algy. He'd just got back from a chess tournament.

'Ollie, I lost again!' he said, and I could see his eyes filling up with tears.

'But that's the second match you've lost this week,' I said.

Algy nodded unhappily. 'It's because you've not been there watching,' he said. 'I never lose when you're there. You're my lucky mascot.' Algy wiped his face with his sleeve. 'Ollie, please. Don't get grounded again. Please don't **Go Bad**.'

'Don't worry, Algy. I won't.'

He smiled. 'Dad says if you're good you can come and watch me in the European Championship Qualifiers on Sunday.'

'**Awesome**!' I replied, trying to sound as excited as I could. 'I'll be there.'

'Thanks, Ollie,' he said, and turned to leave.

'Algy,' I asked gently, 'why did you put **Slimy Stuff** in the twins' ballet slippers?'

He blushed and closed the bedroom door. 'Because they get on my nerves,' he whispered. 'Going on all the time about *pliés* and *passés* and *piqués*.'

'And tutus and *tendus* and *tombés*!' I laughed.

Algy giggled. 'I thought now would be the best time to do it: everyone thinks you've **Gone Bad**, so I knew you'd get the blame. You're

OFFICIALLY GROUNDED anyway, so I didn't think it would matter.'

I grinned at him. 'You're even sneakier than the evil Doctor Devious, in *Agent Q and the* DEMON OF DARKNESS.'

Algy frowned and looked serious. 'Do you think *I'm* **Going Bad** too?' he asked.

'No,' I said. 'And neither am I. Fancy a game of snakes and ladders?'

'Dad says I need to study my new book,

Checkmate! Winning Strategies of the Great Chess Champions,' replied Algy. He opened the door, but then hesitated. 'But I'd rather play snakes and ladders!'

At lunchtime the next day, Peaches pointed at a brightly coloured poster pinned to the noticeboard on the wall nearby:

Competition!

The junior playground is dreary and old.

So let's build a new one that's brilliant and bold.

Design a new playground, amazing and bright,

With excitement and fun, and colour and light!

1st prize: a day out at the zoo

2nd prize: a pencil sharpener

All entries to Mrs Broadside by the last day of the month

'Shall we enter?' asked Peaches. 'I've not been to the ZOO for ages.'

'They've just got a duck-billed platypus,' I said. 'I've always wanted to see one of those.'

I glanced over at the Super And Special table. They were looking at the same poster pinned up on their side of the hall, and Hattie Hurley had already started to write down loads of ideas.

I put my shoulders back and stuck my chest out in a heroic pose. 'The playground is under threat, Special Agent Peaches,' I said.

'This is a job for . . . DEFENDERS OF PLANET EARTH SECURITY.'

Peaches grinned, and undid the straps of her shoulder bag. She chose a pen and pulled a 100 per cent recycled-paper notebook from one of the zip pockets inside. 'Now, what do we want in our new playground?'

We sat quietly for a minute . . .

'A slide,' suggested Peaches, and wrote that down.

'A climbing frame,' I said, and Peaches added that to the list.

'Hopscotch!' she said excitedly. 'We've got to have hopscotch!'

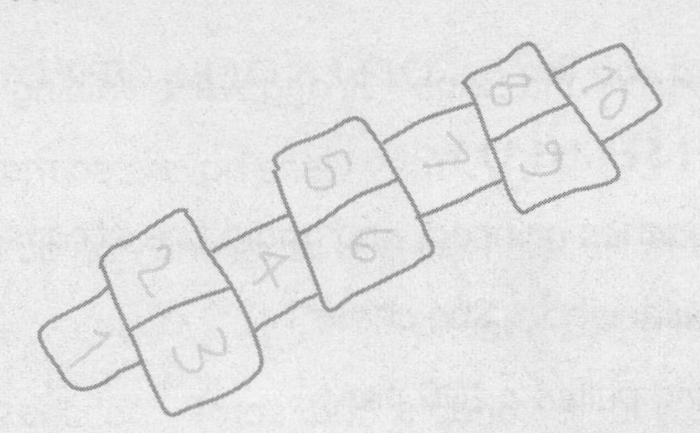

'The trouble is, we've already got all those things,' I said.

'I know that,' answered Peaches. 'I'm just saying we need to keep them. OK, so what else?'

We didn't speak for a minute.

Peaches tapped her teeth with the end of her pen.

We didn't speak for another minute.

The Super And Special kids were making a lot of **noise**. Jamie Ryder and Melody Nightingale were waving their arms around.

Toby Hadron and Bobby Bragg were talking **excitedly**. They were having so many ideas that Hattie Hurley was already on to her third piece of paper.

We added 'sandpit' and 'comfy benches' to our list.

'We've already got those too,' I sighed.

We agreed to think about it over the weekend and add to the list on Monday. Just as the bell went for afternoon classes, Millie Dangerfield sneaked up to me and said, 'Have you had any more exciting adventures this week, Oliver? Did you catch that alien brain?'

Was she winding me up?

A little frown creased her brow, and her eyes were wide with worry.

'I've been having scary dreams about it,' she

whispered, glancing around the playground to make sure no one could hear her. 'Do you think the aliens are taking over everyone, or is it just rocket scientists they're after?'

'Rocket scientists first,' I told her. 'Then the rest of us.'

Millie gasped.

'But don't worry,' I said. 'If anyone can save the world, ***DABMAN*** can.'

Should I do it? I wondered. *Should I tell just one more* ***BIG FAT FIB****?*

No, I couldn't.

Could I?

CHAPTER 6

SHOW AND TELL

Good news: Algy's in the European Finals! Maybe I *am* a lucky mascot after all.

Bad news: I still had to go through **PAIN AND TORTURE** time on Monday morning.

Bobby Bragg told everyone that he'd learned how to chop a brick in half with one blow of his bare hand. He'd even brought a brick in

to school so he could show us. I had to admit it *was* **awesome**. He warned us all not to try it ourselves. As if I needed telling – I may be **Dull And Boring**, but I'm not DUMB AND BRAINLESS!

Toby Hadron had come first in a science competition and won a trip to see the collection of dinosaur fossils at the Museum of Prehistory. He showed us a scary fossilized T-rex tooth he'd been given as a prize.

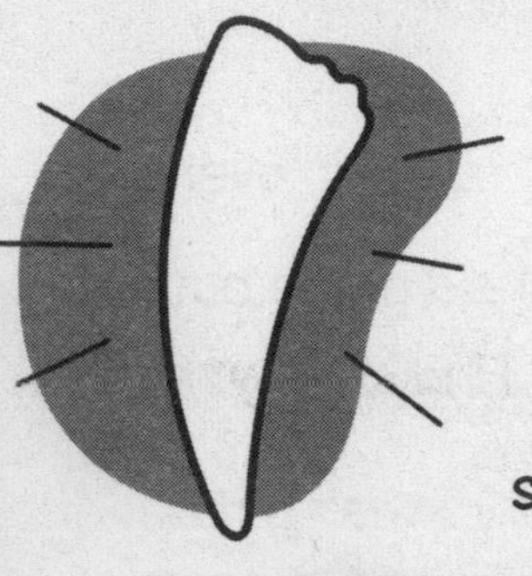

Hattie Hurley said she'd been selected for the Super-Spellers Cheerleading team, and was going to Australia in the summer holidays to compete in the World Championships.

Hattie then showed part of her cheerleading routine, bouncing around at the front of the class, waving red, white and blue pom-poms above her head, and chanting:

> Two, four, six, eight!
> What word do we appreciate?
> D-I-S-C-O-M-B-O-B-U-L-A-T-I-O-N
> Discombobulation!

Peaches told us she'd lost her sun hat over the weekend, and showed us one she'd made out of recycled yogurt pots. (Pea eats gallons of yogurt, because she says it's good for her gut flora – whatever that means!)

Bobby Bragg laughed and said she looked barmy.

Hattie Hurley said she looked bizarre.

I said she looked **BRILLIANT**.

'After last Monday's performance, I hear that Oliver has been grounded all week,' said Miss Wilkins, after calling my name out. 'So I don't suppose he'll have much to **SHOW AND TELL** today.'

She was right – I didn't. As I began to walk to the front of the class, I noticed Peaches frown at me and shake her head. But then I saw Millie Dangerfield's face looking at me, desperate to hear more about the alien brain, and just like last time the words came out before I could stop them.

'At midnight on Tuesday,' I said. 'The brain came back!'

Several of the kids gasped, and glanced nervously at Miss Wilkins.

'Oliver . . .' she growled.

But the pictures were already running through my mind, so I carried on anyway, waving my arms about dramatically.

'Oliver . . .' warned Miss Wilkins.

'It was quivering gently, glowing with a strange green light from the luminous **slime** it had picked up in the drains,' I told the class. 'It was covered in lumps of dark, icky, sticky stuff, and it STANK of . . .'

'I think we can all guess what it stank of, Oliver,' interrupted Miss Wilkins. 'Now go back to your seat . . .'

'Awww, but, miss,' said Millie Dangerfield,

'I want to know what happened!'

Amazingly, shy little Leon Curley put his hand up and said, 'Me too.'

Miss Wilkins sighed. 'Go on then, Oliver, tell us how you escaped from the brain.'

'That can't have taken long,' laughed Bobby Bragg.

Everyone laughed with him. Even Miss Wilkins smiled.

THE ALIEN POINTS AT THE BEDSIDE TABLE.
OOO! A SNIK-SNAK CHOC BAR! MY FAVE!
IT SNATCHES DABMAN'S CHOCCY TREAT AND GOBBLES IT DOWN!
No one steals my Snik-Snak and gets away with it!!
YOU ARE TRULY A DANGEROUS AND BOLD WARRIOR, EARTHLING. YOUR FIGHTING SKILLS WILL BE USEFUL TO US. NOW I WILL TAKE OVER YOUR BRAIN!
DABMAN REACHES AROUND FOR HIS SPECIAL AGENT PEN, BUT IT IS OUT OF HIS REACH ON THE BEDSIDE TABLE.
AGENT Q AND THE BEASTS FROM THE DEEP
HIS FINGERS FIND AN 'AGENT Q AND THE CIRCUS OF HORRORS' COMIC . . .
. . . DABMAN QUICKLY ROLLS IT UP INTO A TUBE . . . BUT THE ALIEN STICKS TIGHT TO HIS HEAD.
THWACK! THWACK! THWACK!

'I felt the cold, **slimy goo** creep into my ears and up my nose,' I said. 'I was seconds away from having a jelly-baby brain.'

'Too late!' shouted Bobby Bragg. 'You've already got one, Oliver Fibbs!'

'Shh!' hissed Millie Dangerfield.

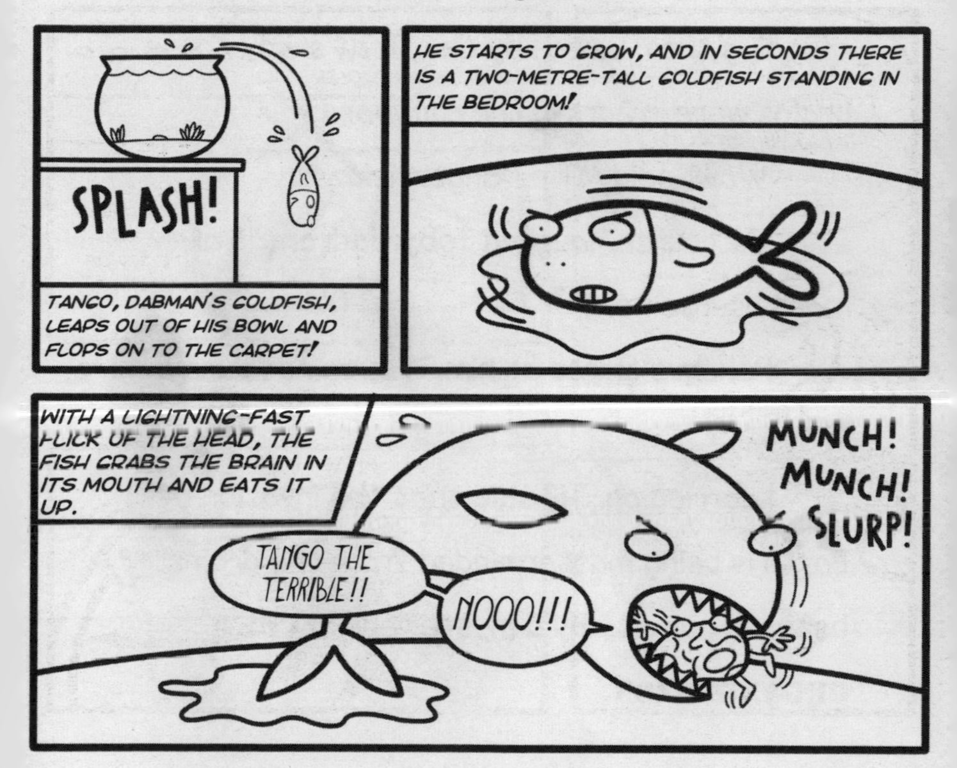

'**EUGHHHHH!**' groaned the class. Hattie Hurley went pale.

'It turns out that my goldfish, Tango, is actually an intergalactic alien hunter from the planet Pondalia.' I explained. 'He's been tracking the alien brains across the Milky Way, and rounding them up one by one. That's why those brains were in jars in the cupboard.'

'Wow!' said Millie Dangerfield.

'Of course,' laughed Toby Hadron. 'It all makes sense now!'

Peaches glared at him. 'You're not funny, Toby.'

I carried on. 'He said that the invasion of Earth is being masterminded from the drains beneath our city by a mysterious **SECRET ORGANIZATION**.'

'Well, children, isn't it amazing what exciting things can happen when you're grounded?' said Miss Wilkins. 'And, Oliver, what have you got to show the class to prove that this actually happened?'

This time, I was ready.

I put my hand in my pocket and took out the blob of luminous green **Slimy Stuff** that Algy had put in the twins' ballet slippers. It dripped and oozed between my fingers.

'This is all that's left of the brain from the drain.'

Hattie Hurley threw up again.

Bobby Bragg shouted, 'Phoney baloney, you make me go groany!'

CHAPTER 7

FLUSHED AWAY

I lost two more **SHINE TIME** points, which took my score down to -3. I also got playtime detention *again*. As the kids in my class rushed and pushed to get out into the playground, some of them were *definitely* looking at me differently.

I sat with Miss Wilkins in the empty classroom, and while she pinned up pictures of **EGYPTIAN** gods for our new history project, I

wrote down the latest instalment of my **BIG FAT FIB.**

It was actually good fun, but as it was supposed to be a punishment I sighed a lot and pretended to look fed-up.

At lunch break that day, I was just tucking into a **BIG DOLLOP** of yummy lasagne, when someone suddenly whispered in my ear: 'Bad things happen to people who tell fibs.'

I jumped with fright, and slopped lasagne down my shirt. I turned, and Bobby Bragg leaned his sneering face so close to mine I could smell the pickled onions he'd had with his lunch.

'They're not fibs,' I said. 'They're . . . stories.'

Bobby snorted. 'Well, they're rubbish stories – **Dull And Boring**, just like you.'

He swaggered over to the **SAS KIDS'** table.

Peaches shook her head, and opened her bag. She unzipped one of the pockets inside, pulled out a packet of tissues and wiped the cheese and tomato from my shirt.

'You need to wash that off when you get home,' she said, taking her notebook out

of the bag. 'If you don't, it'll leave a stain.'

She opened the notebook to the page where we'd been putting our ideas for the playground, and began to read out the list:

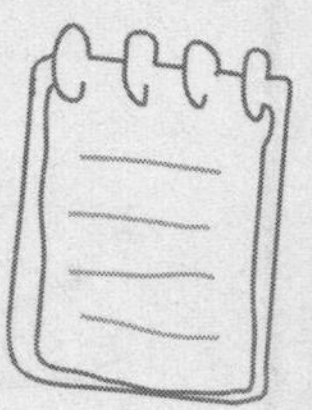

'Slide, climbing frame, hopscotch, sandpit, comfy benches, football goals, basketball hoops, seesaw, roundabout, picnic tables . . .'

Suddenly, a hand reached over her shoulder and snatched the book away.

Bobby Bragg stood over her, grinning as he read the list. 'Is this all you've got?'

Peaches tried to grab the book back, but Bobby held it in the air, out of her reach.

'Hey, gang!' he called to the **SAS KIDS**. 'Listen to this!' Then he read out our ideas in a silly voice. 'Pathetic!' he sneered at the end of it.

Peaches stood up and held her hand out.

'Give it back. That's private.'

Bobby grinned at her, but continued to hold on to the book. 'You might as well give up now,' he said, nodding towards the ***SAS*** table. 'Look.'

They had started making a 3-D model of their playground idea, complete with cardboard trees and cut-out children.

Jamie Ryder hurried over to our table. 'Leave them alone, Bobby,' he said, taking Peaches' book and handing it back to her.

'You're nothing but a great big **SHOW-OFF**, Bobby Bragg,' said Peaches.

'Losers!' he laughed, and swaggered back to his seat.

As I watched him, I thought, **WHAT IF . . .** my **Agent Q** pen could project an anti-gravity

ray at the big jug of custard on the serving counter?

'Take no notice of him,' said Jamie. 'Melody and I have decided to form our own team for the competition. We've all got good ideas, but Bobby Bragg just thinks his are the best.'

He smiled at me. 'Cool **SHOW AND TELL** today, Ollie.'

'Thanks,' I replied.

When Constanza came to school to pick me up (twelve minutes late – she couldn't find the stupido car keys), she looked really worried

as Miss Wilkins told her about my performance that morning. This time, Constanza was frowning like she'd caught a bad case of Crinkly-faced Frowning Disease. I could see that even she was beginning to think I was **Going Bad** like Peter Cowper.

Will I be grounded again? I hoped. No chance. Mum and Dad *really* punished me this time:

'You're banned from reading comics for the whole week!' ordered Mum.

'But what will I do?' I wailed.

'Here's a good idea,' said Dad. 'You can watch the twins rehearse for the ballet on

Saturday afternoon, then go and see them perform in the evening. That'll be fun!'

I wondered, **WHAT IF . . .** the mutant radioactive bacteria had spread from their feet to their whole bodies?

Now *that* would be fun!

On Sunday, I watched Algy compete in his big European Qualifier chess match. He won easily this time. I saw him beam at me and wave, so

I put my thumbs up to congratulate him.

WHAT IF . . . Algy was a **TOP-SECRET** D.O.P.E.S. robot?

When we got home that afternoon, Mum and Constanza were standing together

outside the downstairs bathroom, looking worried and whispering to each other. The sound of the **flushing** toilet filled the hallway. They gasped as we walked in, and I saw Mum try to hide Tango's empty goldfish bowl behind her back.

'Oh! Oliver! You're home early!' she said, flustered.

'Algy won in nineteen moves,' I explained. 'What are you doing? Where's Tango?'

Mum glanced guiltily into the toilet. 'Oliver, I've got some bad news . . .'

'You've flushed Tango down there!' I cried with horror.

Constanza put her arm round my shoulders. 'Oliver, I'm sorry, but your fish goes to heaven when you are out,' she said softly,

speaking in English for once. 'I find him floating – how do you say? – bottom-side up in his bowl.'

'Upside down,' I corrected.

'We got you another one from the Cowpers next door,' said Mum, pointing to a goldfish **SWIMMING** around in a jam jar on the hall table. 'They have a tankful. We didn't think you'd notice the difference.'

I looked at the other fish. 'He's nothing like Tango,' I said.

'Oliver, he's *exactly* like Tango,' said Dad.

'He's not an intergalactic alien hunter from the planet Pondalia, for a start!'

No one spoke. They all looked at me like I'd grown another head. I could almost see the thoughts forming:

I peeked down into the toilet. Suddenly, Tango's body appeared from round the U-bend and floated slowly to the surface of the water.

'He might just be asleep,' said Algy, picking

up the toilet brush and giving Tango a gentle poke.

My goldfish sank a few centimetres into the water, rolled gracefully over and then bobbed back to the surface again. He didn't wake up. There was no doubt about it: Tango was as **DEAD** as the **DEADEST** goldfish you can imagine, times a million.

'Sorry, Ollie,' said Algy.

WHAT IF . . . *I* killed Tango? I wondered.

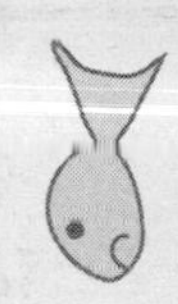

WHAT IF . . . the shock of having a clean fishbowl had given him a heart attack?

WHAT IF . . . the mastermind behind the alien invasion had sneaked up from the drains and poisoned him?

'Goodbye, Tango,' I said, and with a deep sigh flushed the toilet once more. 'Go and save the world.'

There were bright flashes of orange as his little fishy body tumbled in the **bubbling**, churning water, then he was gone. We all peered into the toilet, waiting to see if Tango would float back up again, but this time he'd gone for good.

'I don't want another fish,' I said sadly, and went up to my room.

I studied my collection of **Agent Q** comics, lined up in numerical order on three bookshelves in the corner of my bedroom. I know I was banned from reading them for the weekend, but this was an emergency. I pulled ***Agent Q and the* Beasts from the Deep** from the middle of the second row, and sat on my bed to read it. But for once I couldn't get interested in the story. I kept going over the same strip of pictures again and again, but the words just wouldn't stick in my head.

There was a knock at the door, and Mum came in. I slid the comic quickly under my pillow, and tried to look casual.

'Oliver, I'm really sorry about Tango,' she said, sitting down next to me. 'I didn't realize you were so fond of him.'

'He was my pet,' I said, being careful not to mention the alien-spy-hunter thing again.

'I know, I just never realized you were so interested in fish,' she said.

'I'm *not* interested in fish,' I told her. 'Just Tango.'

'Oh, I see. So there's no point in getting you some books on marine biology then.'

'No.'

Mum sighed and stared at me for ages, while I picked at a loose piece of cotton on my duvet cover, and imagined Tango's body **floating** through the drains and eventually finding its way to sea.

'Oliver,' she said quietly, 'if you could do one thing in the world – anything – what would you want to do?'

I looked at her. 'Anything?'

'Anything.'

'I'd be a **SUPER-SECRET SPECIAL AGENT** working for a **SUPER-SECRET ORGANIZATION** whose sole aim was to save the world from evil and . . . stuff.'

Mum narrowed her eyes a little. 'Apart from that,' she said.

'Read more comics.'

'Oliver, you can't spend the rest of your life reading comics.'

'Why not?'

'Because it's a waste of time,' Mum replied. 'You need to find out what skills you

have, what you're **BRILLIANT** at.'

'Well, I can blow **BUBBLEGUM BUBBLES** as big as a football,' I said. 'Peaches says that's a *spectacular* skill.'

'Yes, I suppose it is,' said Mum. She 

sounded tired. 'Maybe you'll be a star performer with **CIRQUE DU LUNE** one day.'

I grinned. 'That would be cool.'

SHOW AND TELL

PAIN AND TORTURE time was especially bad the next morning.

Bobby Bragg showed us the five gold medals he had won at the inter-schools athletics tournament. Bobby said that Mr Beam, the PE teacher, had said that one day Bobby could be the best athlete the world has ever seen.

Melody Nightingale had sung for world-famous popstar Barry Barlow (which ***is*** pretty spectacular).

Toby Hadron showed us a photo of Saturn he'd taken through his super-duper astronomical telescope at home (I looked hard but couldn't see any aliens).

Peaches had found a potato shaped like a hamster (I thought it looked more like a hippo).

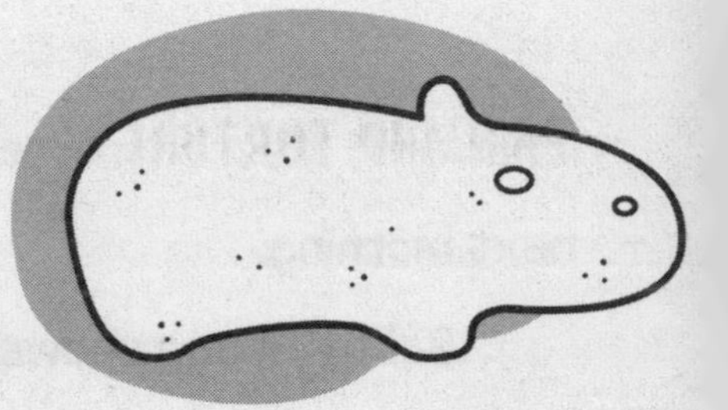

When my turn came, I held up Tango's empty goldfish bowl.

'My goldfish died yesterday.'

All the girls in the class went, 'Awwwww.'

Miss Wilkins looked sad and said, 'I'm really sorry to hear that, Oliver. What happened?'

I did it again.

'He was killed by the EVIL BADDIE who's masterminding the invasion of the Earth,' I replied.

'Oh!' said Miss Wilkins.

I put the bowl on the table and carried on.

'Tango had decided to take the ALIEN brains in jars back to his planet and lock them up,' I said quickly. 'I dressed him in a hat and overcoat and sunglasses, so no one would suspect he was really a two-metre-tall ALIEN hunter from the planet Pondalia. Then we climbed into my Mamba Venom Mark 3 sports car . . .

'Cool car!' said Jamie Ryder.

'Totally!' I agreed. 'Then I pressed the secret rocket activation button on my special pen, and the Mamba transformed into a rocket ship.'

DABMAN AND TANGO BLAST OFF.
INSIDE THE HOSPITAL . . . THE STOREROOM DOORS HAVE BEEN BLASTED OPEN, AND THE BRAINS HAVE GONE!
Pants on fire! They've escaped!
THEY FOLLOW THE SLIMY SPLODGES INTO THE LADIES' TOILETS.
THEY'VE GONE INTO THE DRAINS!
That must be where their secret hideout is!

'There was no time to lose,' I told the class. 'Tango had to go down the toilet.'

'I wish *you* would!' shouted Bobby Bragg.

'Bobby, that's enough!' snapped Miss Wilkins. 'Go on, Oliver.'

'I rushed from the hospital and into the car park. There was a manhole cover in the corner near the building, so I heaved it off, dived down the drain and into the sewers.'

'EUGHHHHH!' went the class.

'In the distance, echoing down the long smelly tunnel, I heard the sound of fighting.'

DABMAN SPLASHES THROUGH THE DRAINS. HE ROUNDS A BEND INTO A HUGE CHAMBER LIT BY BRIGHT LIGHTS . . .
ZAP!
CRASH!
BIFF!
THWACK!
BOOM!
THE RIVER OF SEWAGE WATER RUNS THROUGH THE CENTRE.
The alien command centre!
TANGO!
THE GOLDFISH LIES DEAD ON THE FLOOR . . .
. . . AND STANDING OVER HIS BODY IS SOMEONE DABMAN KNOWS ONLY TOO WELL.
The Show-off!

I saw Peaches' hand fly to her mouth as she giggled and glanced at Bobby Bragg. *She* knew the **SHOW-OFF**'s **SECRET IDENTITY.** Bobby frowned and looked cross – I think he knew it too!

DABMAN'S OLD ENEMY POINTS A ZYGON SUPER NEUTRINO RAY BLASTER ZX5 AT HIM.

It was so quiet in the classroom, you could have heard a beetle burp.

'How did you escape?' whispered Millie Dangerfield.

'I suddenly remembered I had my D.O.P.E.S. pen in my pocket,' I said. 'Quick as a flash, I whipped it out, pressed the anti-gravity button and fired.'

THE SHOW-OFF IS WRAPPED IN A BUBBLE OF ANTI-GRAVITY MATTER, AND BEGINS TO SPIN AND FLOAT TOWARDS THE CEILING.
DABMAN SHOOTS A BEAM OF ENERGY AT THE LIGHT SWITCH ON THE FAR WALL OF THE CHAMBER . . .
THEY ARE PLUNGED INTO TOTAL DARKNESS.
DON'T LET HIM ESCAPE!
Where's the light switch?
I'M AFRAID OF THE DARK!
Get me down!
GOT HIM!
THAT'S ME, YOU IDIOT!
ZAP!
BANG!
BANG!
ARGHHHHHH!

'I grabbed Tango's body . . .'

'But he's two metres tall,' said Bobby Bragg. 'How could you lift him?'

'I told you: his body had shrunk back to goldfish size before he dived down the toilet.'

'Try to keep up, Bobby,' laughed Peaches, and he shot her a furious look.

'Anyway,' I went on, 'using the torch on the end of my D.O.P.E.S. pen, I ran along the tunnel back to the drain but, just when I was nearly free, something grabbed my leg! I kicked hard and slammed the manhole cover down, chopping off the alien's hand! It wriggled on the ground for a

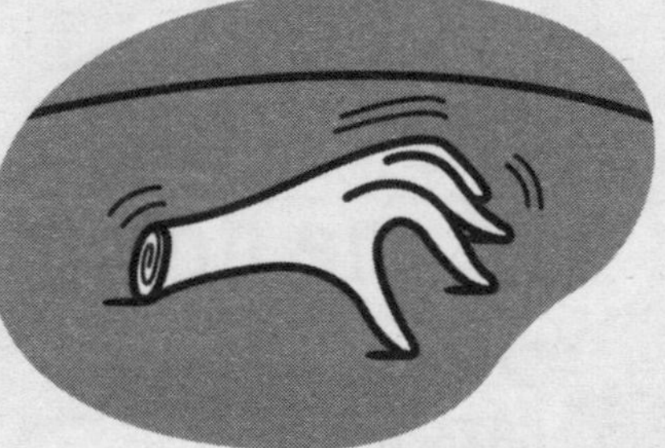

second,' I said, wriggling my own hand to demonstrate, 'and then shrivelled into a wet, messy blob.'

Hattie Hurley covered her mouth and raced from the room.

'What did you do with the fish?' asked Millie Dangerfield.

'I sent him home for a decent burial.'

'Well, Oliver,' said Miss Wilkins. 'What a cliff-hanger!'

'How come you've still got the goldfish bowl if it blasted into space?' said Toby Hadron.

I'd forgotten about the bowl!

'Er . . . the Pondalians sent it back to me,' I replied. 'As a thank-you present for helping Tango.'

Bobby snorted. 'Fake, fake! You eat squashed cake!'

CHAPTER 9

THE BIG IDEA

I got playtime detention again, and wrote down the latest episode of **DABMAN** *and the Attack of the Alien Brain.* For some reason, Miss Wilkins didn't take any more SHINE TIME points off my score. She must have forgotten.

At lunchtime, I sat with Peaches in the school playground, munching on a banana. I stared at the shabby slide, the rusty roundabout and the creaky climbing frame, and

racked my brains for ideas. It was no use; my mind was as EMPTY as the space beyond the edge of the universe.

'The competition closes on Friday,' said Peaches. 'What are we going to do?'

The other kids ran and skipped and hopped, kicking footballs, playing tag, laughing and shouting to each other.

Bobby Bragg was climbing the steps to the

top of the tunnel slide – a long, curling metal tube. He saw me and grinned.

'Look out, Fibbs!' he shouted, pointing at the climbing frame. 'That space rocket has just landed, and it's full of ten-eyed, eight-bottomed, twelve-legged aliens from the planet Biggadiggaboomboom! Better get your dopey pen out and start fighting!'

I tried to ignore him.

'If you need any help, let me know,' he laughed. 'I'm a *real* fighter!'

Bobby showed off a few karate moves, doing a spin-kick and four or five lightning-fast punches, then dived head-first into the dark mouth of the slide.

I thought, **WHAT IF . . .** the tube was

actually a black hole that sucked him into another dimension, where he had to spend the rest of his life fighting *real* ten-eyed, eight-bottomed, twelve-legged **ALIENS** from the planet Biggadiggaboomboom? That would serve him right.

I looked around the playground . . .

And **WHAT IF . . .** the climbing frame really *was* a rocket-ship, and the slide coming off the side was an escape chute?

And **WHAT IF . . .** the roundabout was a S*O*L*A*R* S*Y*S*T*E*M, with planets and comets orbiting the sun?

And **WHAT IF . . .** the picnic tables were actually the control panels of a spaceship?

And **WHAT IF . . .** the soccer goal was the mouth of a **MUTANT MONSTER** from the moons of Jupiter?

I dumped the banana skin into the rubbish bin at my side.

WHAT IF . . . the bin was the atomic fuel cell of a Zygon battle-cruiser?

I jumped up from my seat.

WHAT IF . . . it was really a meteorite shaped like a bench?

'Pea, I've got it!' I said. 'I've got an idea for the playground!'

She took her notebook and pen out of her bag. 'OK, shoot!'

'Aliens!' I said. 'We can transform the stuff that's already here into rocket ships, and comets, and planets and . . . aliens!'

'That's not just an idea, that's a **Big Idea**,' said Peaches. 'In fact, it's a **Whopper**!'

'We'll draw our plans on a big piece of paper, and colour it all in,' I said, 'with pictures of things like the spaceship climbing frame,

so that they know what it'll look like.'

Yikes! I thought. *I'd better stop pretending to read* ***The Complicated Scale Drawings of Nineteenth-Century Engineers,*** *and really start reading it.*

'The trouble is, I'm useless at drawing,' I admitted.

'Let's get the ideas down first,' said Peaches. 'I'll do some doodles in my notebook.'

The bell went for the start of afternoon lessons, but we were having so much **FUN** we didn't notice. Bobby Bragg swaggered past, and glanced at the notebook. Peaches snapped it shut.

'I told you, it's private,' she said.

'I just wanted a good laugh,' sneered Bobby.

Constanza came to pick me up after school. She was nine minutes late today, and shouted, '*Mamma mia! Il telephono! Brrr-brrr! Brrr-brrr! Brrr-brrr!*'

She talked to Miss Wilkins for ages. They kept glancing at me and whispering. I heard the occasional word: evil . . . sad . . . weird and chocolate buttons, but Constanza didn't look worried about me **Going Bad**; in fact, she was laughing and smiling.

When Mum came home from work later on, she and Constanza spoke to each other in Italian.

I thought Constanza would tell Mum about my latest fib, but she seemed to be talking about cats again. Anyway, I didn't get grounded, and I was allowed to read my **Agent Q** comics, so it was back to normal at home.

In fact, it was *more* boring at home than usual.

The twins were dancing in *Swan Lake* all week (no outbreaks of Bothersome Itchy Foot Rot disease).

Algy played chess against his computer every evening, practising for the European Championship Finals at the weekend.

Mum and Dad just got on with their work.

The most exciting thing that happened was when I cut my finger peeling a potato. Mum gave me a tetanus jab, and stuck an **Agent Q** plaster on the cut.

Back at school, I worked hard with Peaches every lunch and playtime, listing our playground plans.

Peaches suggested painting alien bodies on the walls below the Year 4 classroom windows.

'I get it!' I laughed. 'Then when the kids sit at their desks, their heads will match up with the bodies!'

She nodded.

'Year Four aren't human beings, anyway.'

I suggested turning the whole surface of the playground into a universe by painting it with comets and galaxies and planets and stars, and making a huge **BUG-EYED MONSTER** hold up the basketball hoop.

As each day passed, I began to think maybe we *did* have a chance of winning after all.

On Friday morning, Peaches said, 'Is it finished?'

'Is what finished?' I replied.

'The drawing of our playground plan.'

'I thought you were going to do it.'

'No! I thought you were going to do it!'

'I told you, I can't draw a straight line,' I said.

'Neither can I,' said Peaches.

'What are we going to do?' I cried. 'The entries have to be handed in at playtime. We don't have time to do it.'

'We'll just have to hand in my notebook, and hope all my silly doodles are good enough,' said Peaches, with tears in her eyes. 'It won't be the same though,' she added, stomping away to get her bag.

At playtime, I went to see our headteacher, Mrs Broadside. I told her what had happened, and asked if we could put our plans in on Monday morning, in time for the final judging.

'I'm sorry, Oliver,' she replied, 'but there has

to be a deadline. If I give you more time, it wouldn't be fair on the others.'

At lunch, I looked at all the other entries displayed in the hall, and realized how **STUPID** I was to think we stood a chance even if we *had* drawn pictures of our ideas. There were lots of amazing ones. Some kids had stuck pictures from magazines on their plans, while others had used glitter paint.

But the **SAS KIDS** were the only team who had made a **3-D** model. It even had moving parts: the swings swung, the see-saw see-sawed and the roundabout went roundabout. You could even slide little cardboard children down the curling helter-skelter slide.

'It's awesome,' I whispered to Peaches. 'I'd love to have a playground like that.'

'It's OK, but it hasn't got a Big Idea like ours has,' she said sulkily, moving her notebook round to somehow try to make it look more impressive.

I felt as droopy as a popped balloon all weekend. I couldn't even be bothered to read ***Agent Q and the Attack of the Vampire Vikings.***

Then on Sunday Mum, Dad and I all went to the European Championship Chess Finals to watch Algy. Constanza had taken the twins to ballet, of course, to practise their *battlement fondus*, or something like that.

I tried to cheer myself up – you can't be miserable when you're a mascot. Algy was really nervous, so I gave him my last red jelly baby and told him it was my extra-lucky lucky charm, and that it would be like I was sitting in his pocket while he played each game.

'Thanks, Ollie,' he whispered, staring at the sweet just like Professor Lucy Tipping did in **Agent Q and the** *Lost Treasure of the Inca Birdmen*, when she discovered the magical golden bracelet of Pacari-Tampu.

In the hall, I made sure I sat where Algy could

see me when he was playing each game. It was kind of **BORING**, but kind of exciting at the same time. I didn't read a comic – I wanted to be sure my lucky-mascot-ivity was fully focused on my little brother.

It worked! He won! Algy is now the European Junior Chessmaster Champion. How *totally* Super And Special is that? It beats breaking a brick in half with your bare hands any day.

CHAPTER 10

SHOW AND TELL

At **SHOW AND TELL** the next morning, Bobby Bragg told us he could do a backflip, and then showed us. Then he showed us again . . . and again . . . and again.

Millie Dangerfield had been to the premier of the new blockbuster film, ***TOY WARS***, and showed us a photo of her standing next to the ✸star✸ of the movie: her idol, Ritzy Savoy. She even showed us Ritzy's autograph.

Hattie Hurley told us she had come second in the National Spelling Bee Finals, and would have come first, but she had a bit of a **brain-fail** and spelt 'legend' with a j. She showed us her silver medal, and we all clapped.

When it got to my turn, I was going to tell everyone about Algy, and how I'd helped him win, but then Millie Dangerfield put her hand in the air.

'Miss,' she said, 'can Ollie tell us if ***DAB*MAN** defeated the **SHOW-OFF**?'

Miss Wilkins smiled. 'Hands up who would like to hear more of Oliver's story.'

A forest of hands shot up. Bobby Bragg folded his arms across his chest defiantly. Toby and Hattie copied him.

'Very well, Oliver,' said Miss Wilkins. 'But I hope this is the end of your adventure – I don't think I can stand any more excitement.'

I jumped up and went to the front of the class. All eyes were on me. This was my **FINAL FIB.**

'On Sunday, I was ambushed in the kitchen by the **SHOW-OFF** and his army of alien brains,' I began. 'I went for my potato peeler – which is also a hypnotizing ray gun – but before I could press the ON button . . .'

'That's how I got this,' I said. I held up my hand to show the **Agent Q** plaster on my finger.

'I was lucky,' I went on. 'The energy beam

from the **SHOW-OFF**'s blaster had bounced off the ray gun, and hit the **SECRET** rocket activation button on my special D.O.P.E.S. pen.'

I heard Toby Hadron snort with laughter.

'The Mamba Venom Mark 3 zoomed out of the sky,' I said, 'and stopped outside the kitchen window . . .'

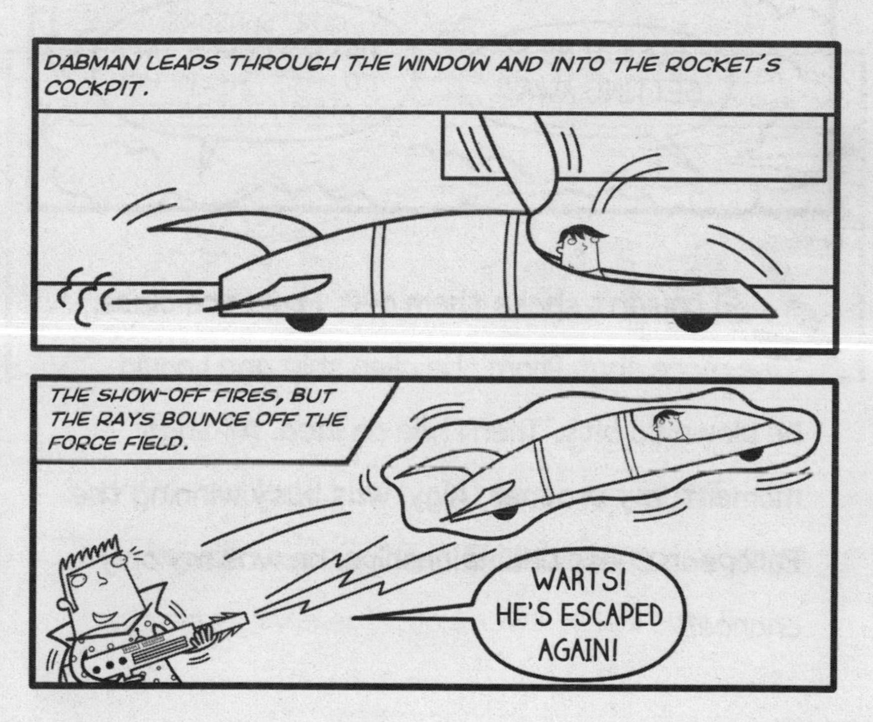

'I couldn't shake them off,' I told the class. 'One more shot from the alien ship and I could be blown to bits. Then I had an idea. At that moment, my brother, Algy, was busy winning the European Chess Championships: he was my only chance!'

THE MAMBA VENOM CRASH-LANDS OUTSIDE THE HALL.
CHESS TOURNAMENT TONIGHT
#1
ALGY! HELP!
NOW MY ALIEN BRAINS WILL TAKE OVER YOUR MIND, DABMAN, AND YOU WILL BE UNDER MY CONTROL!
THE SHOW-OFF AND THE ALIEN BRAINS SURROUND THEM.
NOW EAT HIS BRAIN!
CAN YOU SENSE THE POWER IN THIS BOY'S BRAIN?
IT IS THE BRAINIEST BRAIN WE HAVE FOUND SO FAR!
FEED, BROTHERS!
1

Hattie Hurley guessed what was coming next. Her hands flew to her ears (they didn't *actually* fly – she's not *that* Super And Special!). She screwed her face up, and began to make little squeaky noises – like a mouse with hiccups – so she wouldn't hear.

'There were bits of brains everywhere,' I said. 'It was like an explosion in a jelly and custard factory.'

'EUGHHHHH!' went the class.

'Algy had absorbed all their power and

knowledge,' I said. 'He knew their attack plans – the Earth was saved!'

'What about the **SHOW-OFF**?' asked Millie Dangerfield.

'He was so shocked at seeing the brains explode,' I replied, 'that he didn't see me sneak up on him. I knocked the blaster from his hand and . . .'

Miss Wilkins stood up and said, 'Hooray! We can all sleep safe in our beds thanks to Oliver Tibbs – or should I say DABMAN!'

Everyone cheered and clapped, except Bobby Bragg, of course.

'And don't forget,' she said, 'the teachers will be judging the playground competition at lunchtime. There will be a special assembly straight after lunch to announce the winners.'

A buzz of excitement buzzed around the class. Who would go to the ZOO, and who would get the pencil sharpener?

CHAPTER 11

THE RESULT

At lunchtime, everyone went to the hall to check that their entries looked as good as possible before the judging began. Peaches and I just needed to make sure that the notebook was open at the right page.

There was an empty space on the table where it should have been.

'Where is it?' I cried as we searched desperately around the display board,

under the tables and behind all the other entries.

'It's been stolen!' cried Peaches.

Bobby Bragg stood with the **SAS KIDS** around their fantastic model. He raised one eyebrow and smirked at us.

'So you decided to take your entry out of the competition,' he said. 'Good to see you know when you're beaten.' He laughed, and nudged Hattie Hurley. 'Or maybe the aliens took it!'

'Pea, maybe it's for the best,' I said. 'It was a rubbish entry.'

'I'm not giving up that easily,' said Peaches, looking daggers at Bobby.

She opened her bag and began to rummage inside. 'I had a feeling something like this might happen,' she said, taking out another 100 per cent recycled paper notebook, identical to the first. 'So it's a good job I made a copy.'

'Pea!' I cried. 'You're so . . . sensible!'

'I make copies of everything – just in case.'

Bobby Bragg scowled at her as she opened the book and placed it on the table. 'You still won't win,' he spat. 'Ours is a trillion times better than yours.'

'OK, everyone out!' shouted Mrs Broadside. 'Let the judging begin!'

I couldn't eat anything at lunchtime, not even the chocolate pudding. My stomach felt as though it was full of the Wriggling Weebie Worms that infected **Agent Q** in ***Agent Q and the JUNGLE OF CREEPING DEATH***.

At the special assembly straight after lunch, Mrs Broadside kept us waiting while she made some other announcements about the library, and litter, and a lost sock.

'Well,' she said eventually, 'I suppose you all want to know which entry the teachers have picked as the best design for our new playground.'

'Yes!' we all shouted.

The headteacher smiled, then said some stuff about how hard it had been to choose, and how the entries were all very different, but all very good, and then she said, 'One was really outstanding, and that was the excellent model by Year Six pupils Bobby Bragg, Hattie Hurley and Toby Hadron.'

Everyone began to clap. My heart ❤ seemed to drop ❤ to my feet.

'Yesssssss!' hissed Bobby, and shuffled along the line of kids with the other two to get his prize. As he passed me, he gave me a nudge in the back with his knee.

What if the D.O.P.E.S. Command Spaceship beamed me up at that moment, so I wouldn't have to listen to him crowing about winning?

Mrs Broadside shook their hands, then gave them each a pencil sharpener.

Bobby Bragg realized what was happening at the same time I did, and I saw his grin fade instantly: the pencil sharpener was the *second* prize!

'Well done, you three,' said Mrs Broadside. 'Your ideas were excellent, your model was **BRILLIANT** and your design had modern, state-of-the-art equipment, however . . .'

She turned to the rest of us.

'There was one entry that was *especially* clever,' she said. 'It has an amazing, original theme of space travel. The children who did it obviously put a great deal of hard work and imagination into coming up with some fantastic ideas, and illustrated them with oodles of doodles. In this playground, every

playtime will be an adventure: you'll be able to hop across galaxies when you play hopscotch, feed the gaping mouths of hungry litter-aliens with your rubbish, and take the controls of an INTER-GALACTIC SPACE cruiser after your lunch!'

The kids in the hall laughed and began to chatter excitedly.

'But what's *really* great about this idea,' Mrs Broadside went on, 'is that it uses everything that's already in the playground, and makes it even better. We'll be saving the planet in two ways: recycling the old equipment, *and* fighting children-chomping alien invaders!'

Then Mrs Broadside held up Peaches' notebook.

'So the teachers and I have decided that the first prize goes to this wonderfully imaginative and ingenious entry from Peaches Mazimba and Oliver Tibbs!'

Everyone cheered and clapped as the two of us made our way to the front of the hall.

WHAT IF . . . this was all just a dream, and I suddenly woke up to find Bobby Bragg in top place, as usual?

As I stood in front of the assembly, looking at the First Prize certificate, and the vouchers saying FREE PASS TO THE ZOO, I realized it was true: we'd won the competition. Our alien adventure idea was going to be turned into a real playground.

Back in class, Miss Wilkins said that we

should have a *special* **SHOW AND TELL** – just me and Peaches telling the class how we came up with our design.

Bobby Bragg's hand shot into the air. 'Miss, I want to show everyone how I can chop through a brick.'

'You showed us that two weeks ago, Bobby,' said Miss Wilkins. 'Come to the front, please, competition winners.'

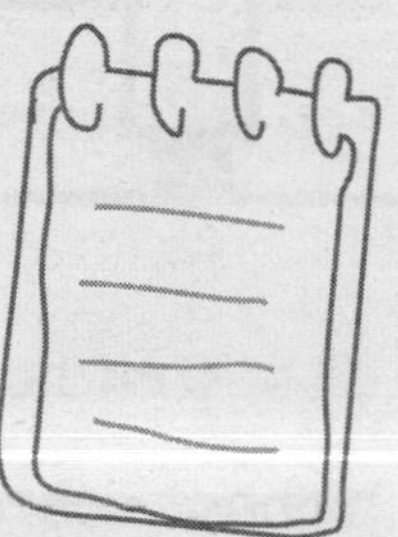

Peaches and I told the class about our **Big Idea**, holding open the notebook and pointing to the pages as we talked. When we finished, the class cheered and clapped again.

'I'm going to award Oliver and Peaches ten SHINE TIME points each,' said Miss Wilkins.

That rocke**ted** me from -3 to +7. My highest score ever! I couldn't wait to get home and tell Mum, Dad and Algy – there was no way even Emma and Gemma would think I was **Going Bad** after this.

'Cool idea!' said Jamie Ryder, and held up

his hand to high-five me as I walked back to my desk.

Bobby Bragg tossed his second-prize pencil sharpener in the air, and stared at me with cold, fierce eyes. Lucky for us he didn't have a Zygon Super Neutrino Ray Blaster ZX5 at that moment, or he'd have **zapped** me and Peaches into a trillion zillion atoms.

I couldn't wait to get home and tell my mum and dad what I'd done, but Constanza was twenty minutes late picking me up. '*Stupido!*' she cried, kicking the front tyre of the car before she got in it. '*Pop!*' she yelled, throwing her hands in the air to demonstrate a tyre bursting.

When I showed Constanza the certificate and voucher, she threw her hands in the air again, shouted, '*Bravo! Magnifico!*' and gave me big sloppy kisses on both cheeks.

I climbed into the front seat of the car. The twins were discussing their new (**Slime**-free) ballet slippers.

'I've won a trip to the **ZOO**!' I said.

'Well, we're going to the National Ballet,' said Emma.

'To see Dame Elizabeth De Ath in *Swan Lake*,' added Gemma.

When I told Algy, though, he was incredibly jealous. 'Can I come too?' he asked. 'I want to see the platypussies.'

'Sorry, Algy, the prize is for me and Peaches only,' I replied. 'But I promise I'll buy you a *wind-up* platypus from the gift shop.'

Mum and Dad were overjoyed at my news.

'Maybe you *are* going to be a **BRILLIANT** engineer after all, Oliver,' said Mum.

'Or an architect, like me,' beamed Dad.

'I didn't *engineer* the playground – I just had a **Big Idea**,' I told them, but they weren't listening.

'I've got some tremendously interesting books on building design that you can read, Oliver,' said Dad.

'Are they really big books?' I asked.

'**Huge**,' he answered, running into his office and coming back with a **MONSTER** volume of *Fundamental Principles of Architecture: How*

to make sure your building doesn't fall down.

'Fantastic,' I said, realizing that it was so big I could easily hide an **Agent Q** comic inside. In fact, it was so humongous I could hide *two* comics inside, maybe even THREE!

CHAPTER 12

DABS ARE GO!

At lunchtime the next day, Peaches and I bought chocolate-chip muffins to celebrate our win.

`Would you like to be in my next story, Pea?' I asked her. `Fighting monsters, discovering **SECRET** treasure, spying on evil scientists . . .' An idea flashed into my mind. `**WHAT IF . . .** the two of us were a pair of **TOP-TOP-SECRET** D.O.P.E.S.?'

Peaches sighed, and shook her head.

'**WHAT IF . . .** we were DABS? **Dull And Boring** Superheroes!' I stuck out my chest, and raised my chin. 'I, of course, am ***DABMAN!***'

Peaches rolled her eyes. 'I don't know about **TOP-TOP-SECRET** – you are Top-Top-Silly,' she said. 'Can we get back to planning our trip to the **ZOO**?'

'Sorry, Pea,' I said. 'If you're in my ***DAB*** Gang, you have to have a Super Identity.' Before she could complain, I said, 'Peaches Mazimba, I hereby

appoint you . . . **Captain Common Sense**, with the Power of Being Sensible.'

Peaches sighed again, and shook her head, but she was smiling too.

The bell rang for the start of afternoon classes. As we began to clear away our trays, Bobby Bragg blocked our path. Toby Hadron and Hattie Hurley stood by the door.

'*We* should have won that competition,' said Bobby. 'Your entry was **Dull And Boring**, just like you. Ours was miles better.'

'I liked their idea, actually,' said Hattie.

'Yeah,' said Toby, 'It was . . .'

Bobby glared at them, and they shut up straight away.

Suddenly I thought, **WHAT IF** . . . the **SHOW-OFF** had got a gang of superheroes under mind control, and he was using them as slaves to do his dirty work for him.

I smiled at the picture in my head.

'You think you're clever, don't you, Fibbs?' said Bobby Bragg.

I looked into his eyes. I could tell that at that moment he saw me as a great big lump of brick that he wanted to karate chop into a million pieces. He didn't say it, but I knew what he was thinking:

Bobby Bragg may have his Killer Karate Chops, but I had my ***Big Fat Fibs.***

I'M OLIVER, DEFENDER OF PLANET EARTH. BUT BEFORE I CAN SAVE THE WORLD I MUST ESCAPE THE GIANT BOY-MUNCHING BUGS!

LIAR, LIAR, PANTS ON FIRE!

It's true. If they bite me they'll give me the dreaded Wenghi Benghi fever – I'll break out in a green rash and radioactive spots and – OK, maybe I'm exaggerating . . .

But as I keep telling everyone,

THEY'RE NOT FIBS, THEY'RE STORIES!

DANNY BAKER
RECORD BREAKER

STEVE HARTLEY

DANNY BAKER RECORD BREAKER
THE WORLD'S BIGGEST BOGEY
STEVE HARTLEY
DANNY BAKER RECORD BREAKER
THE WORLD'S AWESOMEST AIR-BARF
STEVE HARTLEY
DANNY BAKER RECORD BREAKER
THE WORLD'S LOUDEST ARMPIT FART
STEVE HARTLEY
DANNY BAKER RECORD BREAKER
THE WORLD'S STICKIEST EARWAX
STEVE HARTLEY
DANNY BAKER RECORD BREAKER
THE WORLD'S ITCHIEST PANTS
STEVE HARTLEY
DANNY BAKER RECORD BREAKER
THE WORLD'S WINDIEST BABY
BURP!
PARP!
STEVE HARTLEY

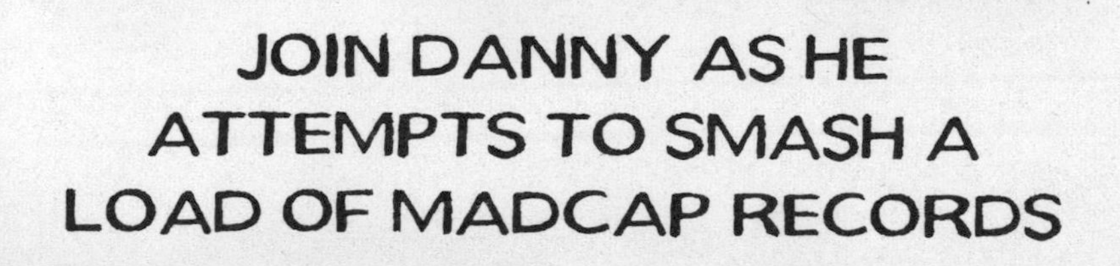
JOIN DANNY AS HE
ATTEMPTS TO SMASH A
LOAD OF MADCAP RECORDS